Rising From
The Roots

Jasmine Farrell

Cover artist: Rabia Aamir
ISBN: 978-1-7379460-7-6
www.jasminefarrell.com

This book is dedicated to:
Grit, my loved ones and those who have
supported me along my journey.
Oh...and French fries.

Acknowledgements

I would like to thank my father for being so supportive of me and my dreams. He has been an ear, voice of reason, and solid source of wisdom when I forget sense sometimes. His patience, grace and willingness to have an open mind has often inspired me to do the same. This book, any book of mine for that matter wouldn't have been published without him in my corner. I'm proud to have a father like him! Let that man eat an apple in my presence... I always want a slice or 3. ALWAYS.

I also want to acknowledge my mother. I carry her strength, grit, and resilience within me. The way I craft my pieces reflects her influence. She was the first to introduce me to poetry, and when I began performing spoken word in my early twenties, she encouraged me to never hold back.

My spouse, Reign, deserves special thanks. I appreciate their support, the delicious memories we create, and their patience. My early morning lines or late-night memo pad jots love when Reign checks them out! My honey bun with the extra glaze, Reign has been rooting for me since the beginning. And let's not forget—have you seen their smile? Sheesh! I'm grateful to wake up to their beautiful brown eyes. The story behind those stunning irises is poetry all by themselves. I wish us more adventures and late-night giggles.

I want to acknowledge my Auntie Mo. Her encouragement, kindness, laughter, and love have propelled me forward. The space she has created for me to simply be myself is truly humbling.

My longtime soul sista, Dominique is a blessing that I wish we all had in our lives. Their friendship, sisterhood and care has kept me steady throughout the years. From Jr. high to future old ladies with flava, I hope we continue to flourish in each other's lives.

To my loved ones who embrace all parts of me without hesitation: thank you. Whether near or far, whether we spoke yesterday or years ago, I cherish you all.

Lastly, I'm grateful for music; it lifts me during the tough times and elevates my spirit on the good days.

Table of Contents

Reader's Note

Hi and stuff!

If this is the first project of mine you've read, thank you for snaggin' it.

If you're returning, welcome back! I missed ya'll and stuff. I appreciate your continued support. :)

10 years...a decade of my life—challenging my upbringing, deconstructing beliefs, rediscovering myself, and facing my inner battles. I've embraced my journey, unlearning and relearning along the way, cutting off unhealthy habits, mindsets, and even people. The core of it all? Authenticity.

It hasn't been easy. I've stumbled and tripped more times than I can count, but each fall has taught me something valuable. Whether you've read my poetry collections, poetry series, or a fictional project, if my words have made you feel understood, uplifted, challenged, or even annoyed, thank you for giving them a chance.

At this stage in my life, I'm feeling thankful that I made the hard choices and dropped the ball for the sake of my peace and self-respect. I'm grateful for the love I'm surrounded by, the love I enjoy giving, the fucks I no longer have, my

11

supporters, my ambition and lifelong commitment to writing my lil' ol' poems and creating. I'm proud of how far I've come and where I'm going. Whether I'm eating ramen noodles and coffee or talking with my hands with colorful tips...or crying about a winter that feels as though it's taking over me, or feeling so elevated that I'm besties with a nimbostratus: I'm good.

I've learned to appreciate the beauty of balance— the deep ebbs and smooth flows of existence. Letting my roots remind me of how far I've come and allowing my wings to push me higher.

Thanks again for reading and stuff.

Your support means the world.

Roots

Being Alive

I didn't get lost in the shadows.
As a wanderer, I've always found it.
Unafraid of the darkness, the unseen.
Strolled in the unforeseen
knowing
the light would pass by with a wave and a new
route.
You know…
                    Life.

Exploring light, looking into darkness.
Finding joy in both.
                    Knowing
there is peace in both.
You know…
                    Being alive, my dear.

Moving Lips, Idle Legs

Frozen in time.
Suspended in your misery.
Fussing to yourself at the starting line
while I've been running
this marathon with my chest out,
running this marathon,
hopping over hurdles,
running this marathon,
sludging through the mud.

Running this marathon without a raincoat,
running this marathon without sneakers.
Just geared up with ambition.

Honey, you could never.
You would never.
You're too busy
talking shit at the starting line...
    STILL.

In My Element

Life had a way of eating away at my flesh
'til I was a size 2.
I lost the fear of death at age 23, in summer.
By October of that year, I reunited with the dark,
inviting foreign shadows for a night on the town
where laughter masked the echoes of solitude.

Nothing frightened me anymore,
except the thought of my words
remaining unheard, trapped in silence.
Then I published something.

And I wouldn't stop—
each word a step toward liberation,
each line a testament to my resilience.

Unshacklin'

I used to carry it beneath my chest—
ain't nothin' hollow about a weight
that pulls you deeper into the ground
when a majestic transformation beckons you to
rise.
Why bother?
The past is a familiar comfort,
a faithful bully chasing me in common shadows.
Ain't nothin' hollow about a weight
that solidifies my fears.
Why bother?

Some aches take years,
some betrayals never fade like sand
on low-level boardwalks.
I know what it's like to carry a boulder
that was never mine to bear.
It's no one's to carry.

So, I bother.
I bother to challenge the voice
that tries to smother my light,
to face my fears and say,
"Get behind me. The lessons are my
foundation."
The present is mine.
Forward looks good on my essence.

Ain't nothin' hollow about deceit,
but neither is my strength—
my tenacity.

Daring to Flourish

I got sick of apologizing
after they chipped away at my essence,
munching away at my spirit with every careless
word,
taking actions that were absolutely absurd.

So, I kicked them off my square
daring them to return with katana in hand,
ready for the fight they never saw coming.

They shouldn't even think about it.

I already saw the mask slip,
the lovely façade crumbling like worn paint.
Might as well take it completely off if we happen
to cross paths again.
I'll be sure to stand tall and reveal the vibrant
pieces they thought would wither,
the roots they believed would never grow
another.
Watch as I blossom in defiance,
stronger than before,
rising from the shadows.

Hey, Honey.

People love you in one moment
and forget about you in the next.

Who wants to remember the person
who stabbed them in the back
after being just being embraced by the same
being?

Sincerely,
A former friend who thankfully got away.

Endurance

The sun sulks where I am.
No invitation for fresh air and easy walks down
clean streets where I am.

I want a serene space without fight.
A heavy hand of ease, a light breeze,
laughter to fill in the space between.

There is a chill that I haven't felt in a while,
breaking motivation by the root.
I battle against the ultimate crumble.
I will not disintegrate this momentum.

There is a season up yonder.
A shift that pulls me up out of the uncertainty.

The suffering is within the patience.
I wail in the waiting.
Anxiously watching in the sorrows.
Peeking for hints to light up my eyes to keep
going.

All I have is the dream.
All I have is the taste of love on my lips
and infinity in my heart,
my ancestors rubbing the knots out of my spirit.
Me and the sun finna warm up and rise soon.
It's the wailing in the waiting right now.
That will change soon.

It will…

Closure-less

She was wrapped up in that curly phone wire,
leaning on the kitchen doorway,
searching for open arms; her ear awaited,
                              hoping for good news.

Sat on the twin mattress,
I hummed a tune,
calming the need to carry more of her story.
It was heavy.
Repressing my lines felt heavier.

Everybody told me to grin and bear it.
So, I grinned,
bearing the weight under my long jean skirt.

She is still wrapped up in that curly phone wire.
Crying over Carol, fussin' over Katrina, laughing
with Drew, sobbing over Maddy and mourning
over Ru.
I overstand.
That's why I stayed for so long—
It took me awhile to realize just how much of a
problem that was.

So wrapped in her story,
I forgot I had my own.
She ended up writing mine for me
while I carried hers.

Is that codependence?
Manipulation with a prayer shawl of obligation?
I'll never know.
I left the twin mattress,
stopped humming
and snatched my story back.

And, no—
I am not waiting around for restitution.

Put the Gay in the Trunk

Naomi's mother is a powerful woman
with the heart the size of a Buick.
When she found out
that her daughter's soul
adores the smiles of women,
the empty seats were suddenly occupied
with a haunting nothingness.
"No seats left."
So, she motioned for Naomi
to sit in the trunk
with the rest of the unmentionables:
The dreams denied,
the love unspoken.

I Been Whole...I Just Forgot

Fourteen and clawing to be free,
besties, both raised in Pentecostal glee.
Punky, alternative dork,
flailing my hands in fishnet gloves,
groomed as a dove, yet born a phoenix.

You were anchored in righteous wisdom
from "the Good Book."
After school, we'd giggle over the phone,
sharing secrets of church affairs
and our "When I Grow Up" dreams.

One day, I summoned you
beneath the tree of secrets,
crafting a sacred note
about attractions—
there was a girl…
At the end of the school year,
I found myself on the phone,
crying in the kitchen,
heartbroken after learning you told.
Confused about what is and what ain't.
(What the hell is comphet anyway?)
Will Mama find out?

Two years later, I prayed for deliverance,
asking for a change,
for God to fix me into
the good, pretty, well-mannered,

dick-loving woman
I was supposed to be.
I did well for a while…
But in the end,
that God didn't hear me.
Another one did.

From the roots,
a divine voice whispered,
"You are enough, just as you are."
No longer bound by shame,
I embraced the truth of my heart,
roots intertwined with love and strength.
On this journey, I am whole;
I always was.
No longer seeking to fit into a mold,
but celebrating the vibrant spectrum
of who I'm meant to be—
just lil' ol' me.

Fleeting Canvas

During the early spring of 2016, I saw you.
Your shoulders swayed on the B43,
sandwiched between him and your little sister.
She got so big!
I locked eyes with you;
your gaze fell to his polished shoes—
good quality, patent brown leather with mustard
laces.

You were my scissor partner,
a secret Santa gift from someone's gods.
I remember the aroma of
shea butter and sugar melon lingering
long after you left Haki's room.

I closed my eyes, listening to the bus hum,
racing past local stops, trying to forget
how you made my heart pause, then flutter,
at the sight of your dimples after a swim.
I tried to forget those pointy-toed shoes,
the skinny four-inch heels highlighting your
gorgeous legs.
I tried to.

Faded memories you deny exist—
"I'm delivered," you said back in 2014,
your head held high to the heavens,
where I'm apparently not allowed in.
You've forgotten me—every kiss, caress,

and shared appetizer,
a figment of my imagination,
because your family finds it best,
because it blemished your image.
So you painted over it,
hoping the old paint won't bleed through,
hoping the new paint won't chip off.

Yeah...
        I get it...
                I've been there...
                        I was delivered once...

Waiting for the Good Part

I ache but I yearn.
Anticipate for that reason for the ache.
For that reason, *for* this struggle.

Can someone bread crumb me to better days?
Lead me the section where ease and joy carry me
the rest of the way.

Rest has left me and sleep is a phony companion.
My body is the proof.
My dark circles give evidence.
Can someone snag me out of this?

Trust

Thoughts of how I left my determination,
my unclothed voice and autonomy by the
wayside
long enough.
Told my barebones to whisper while I'm poorly
postured
long enough.

You are waiting for me to open up,
to shed my plastered iron
and share my safe keeping.

Baby, is you crazy?

Women like me were groomed
to talk a little higher,
hush a little longer
and prove our worthiness
to well-meaning snagglefolk.

Baby, my safe keeping will flock to you
when it's ready.

You finna wait?

D Be Lyin'

You watched yourself sink down
into a hole you've plunged into before.
Now self-sabotage has you captive.
Winter craves you as its new hostage.
Remember the joy that permeated your insides,
spilling onto the hard soil of self-doubt.
Remember the first time you found your thing—
and clarity kissed your forehead,
"Good morning."

This is beyond personification.
Lovely, I'm asking you to fight this.
I know that hole got you feeling lonely.
The dirt walls make it hard to climb,
and you think you might be sinking deeper
just by standing still.

Suddenly, there's a chill…
a whisper of cold words you've heard before.
But think farther back—to the time
your loved one wrapped their arms around you
so tight,
love sparked from you first,
then flowed into their arms.

Lovely, I'm asking you to look up.
You are not solo.
You and Lonely have nothing in common.
Look up.

They are a shout away.
A text away.
A call away.
They are there.
Just look up.
Let them help you out of that hole.

Penalty

The cloud dissipated— you've been revealed.
Thought you could stay hidden forever,
but the fog is gone, honey— you are exposed.
Face card declined but that fake smile will be
compensated.
Soul is over drafted; your fate has been
designated.
No amount of dead trees painted green will turn
this punishment into a dream.
Betted against me, hoping I'd never wise up.
Should've ceased at the warning.
TIME'S UP.

Vanquish

Four skeletal fingertips press against my temple
while slumbering.
Who can sense a chill
while occupied in dreamland?

The crunching and crackling of what's left of you
waits for the haunting to settle within my
thoughts.

An execrable award
for rising to the occasion,
revealing the faux peacock's identity:
                        The child of the grim reaper.

Yet, I, a phoenix, have died 1,000 deaths
and
will rise once more—
1,001.

Reckoning

Phone was off for days, bills were due.
Her pen kept moving,
she was still pushing through.
Built up grit makes the flavor linger a little
longer.
A force in hibernation and you chose to wrong
her?
Did you hear the gong?
Get off the floor, your performance is over.
Hope you got the exposure you wanted.
Heard you paid the promoter well.
A job well done with your wickedness.
Typical clientele to mindlessness.
Your higher light weeps,
knowing your integrity, you didn't keep.
Did you hear the gong?
What you sowed...is ready to be reaped.
Keep your concession, she doesn't need your
confession.
Your malicious supporters have left you
defenseless.

Accession

Not nary a weight can crash my flight.
No dark magic can sniff my light.
I'm free in this skin.
Love my flava from within.
I know where the sauce comes from too.
Dem prayer warriors and preachers,
uttering Psalms on cue.
Fiery hearts that beat to selah.
I know where sauce comes from.
Dem witches and warlocks that unbind,
remove the green snake eyes and evil ones too.
My steps are heavy from the fusion
lineage.
Ain't scared of where I come from.

You can't stop this journey.
You won't cease the yearning,
the overflowing ambition,
the consistent intuition,
the evolution of self,
the annihilation of self-sabotage.
This
   growth
      got
        muscle.

Past agony turned into endurance.
My lane can't be touched.
Ain't no competition,

I ain't lookin-
this is for myself.

A friend reminded me
to take my destiny off the shelf.
So, I'm here:
Walkin heavy,
talkin' deeply,
not givin' a fuck who sleepin'.
Suga, this woman got bass and all that shade-
you can keep it.

I'm free in my skin.
Love my flava from within.
My purpose sittin' pretty underneath my
footsteps.

I've seen enough to know,
fate flows under every path I take.
Just wait.

Grateful Goodbye

I'm thankful you soared straight to the rainbow,
bypassing our beings on this plane.
Your absence solidified the freedom I craved
and that person's aftermath intentions.
I hope the colors amaze you,
magnetizes your essences to grow in might so
divine,
the ethereal double takes at your size,
knowing you ain't nothin' to play with.

Your loss solidified the truth
that some endings have a process of complete
annihilation...
For just in case there is a glimmer, a miniscule
enticement to look back at misery.

Your loss freed you from being weaponized
as an entrapment,
a hunter of dreams
and killer of spirits.

You were destined to ignite purpose,
pull sleeping spirits out of hibernations and
cowardice wounds.

You aimed towards the strip of yellow and green,
made it a home,
knowing how monumental you are.
And, I'm so thankful you did.

Your absence solidified that although I was detoured,
my journey continues on the right path.
I love you.

Thread Ashes Blowing in the Wind

We connected at the pain.
Attached at the hip from the bullying we endured
growing up.
Tethered by awkwardness,
we tussled with your desire for me to be
something I wasn't.
I told you I wasn't.
But I tried to be the "was" you wanted me to be.

Artificial acceptance has always been an enemy
to me.
A phony idea airplaned to open my mouth
and chew in order to control my being
ever since I was a wee thing.

I *knew* better.
But
I *chose* worse.

Honey,
worse tore my ass up
better than my mama ever could.

Faux acceptance has always been an enemy of
mine.
We are an enemy of mine.
You are an enemy of mine.
I am a friend, supporter, comforter—
AI from day one of mine.

41

Grateful I severed the tie
and burned the string to ash
for good measure.

We linked at our brokenness.
Eventually, the cause for each other's crumbling.
We became rubble.
Mutual annihilation.

I hope you rebuilt as well as I did.
Or, better.

Acceptance Part 4

I didn't just wake up one day and chose it.
After years of brainwashing, self-loathing,
praying for deliverance,
slipping, falling, striving to be whole,
gritting my teeth,
holding hands that make me think of everything
else but the moment:
I surrendered to it.
Gave true acceptance a chance.
Peace overtook me.
I didn't just wake up one day and chose it.
It was always there.
I finally found the right pair of eyes to properly
see,
to unpack and rediscover
pieces of myself long lost.

Salt in the Morning

A cozy room,
a wealthy Saturday morning,
an abundance of recovery from last night's
shenanigans.
I wondered…
Does she ever think about me?

Cotton shorts gripped my skin,
your hands preoccupied—
a gathering of firm fingers around my waist.
I knew then you'd give me hell if I ever let you
go,
but I didn't foresee the moment
when I'd have to.

Looking back, I thought your sass
might keep my hunger at bay.
I was certain your hair flips and tongue clicks
could distract me
from what I actually craved.

Your breath tickled the side of my neck, and I
wondered…
Will I ever see her again?

I breathed in your salt,
your funk,
your masculinity—
hoping it would fill the empty pockets in my

belly.
I breathed you in—with obligation.

Besides,
Ina was married
and told me my head was too deep in the clouds.
But there ain't nothing wrong with a cocktail of
cirrus and deep ruminations.

You shiver and exhale.
"Good morning, you."
"Hey, baby."
"IHOP?"
"Yeah."

Life goes on, I guess.

Journal Entry #7097

Shadow thoughts in this July heat.
Discreet revelations simmer on the window sill
and I coulda slapped that people-pleasing-
jitterbug right then and there out the window...
For allowing myself to stay that long.
For allowing myself to be connected in the first
place.

Shadow thoughts in this July heat.
I meet my higher self for the upteempth time to
tell me to release.
So, I release.

Desperation's Petals

I used to let the unknown conjure desperation
from the depths of my shadows, forcing it down,
sprinkling pretty roses above,
hoping that romanticizing my avoidance
would somehow ease the sting of trust.
But one day, life swept the roses aside,
flinging my true feelings over its shoulder,
laughing at my involuntary nakedness.

Trust the process, y'all...

Bullies in their Good Clothes

Peace doesn't recognize you
because you've been playfighting
with chaos all these years.
Hair tangled from entertaining gossip junkies,
cracked out on misery.
You used to siphon smiles
from those you claimed to admire
because glee and exuberance
ran away at the hint of your essence.

Your creativity has shown the opposite,
Utilizing verbal descriptive imagery
and visual acrostics to metaphorically pen
the beauty of kindness.

Whole time you act like a Gretchen or Edgar
from 6th grade,
Favoring Chris Hargensen in school.

Dear mean girl with responsibilities:
Be still.

Healing ain't THAT scary.
Owning up to your actions
Won't conjure up Nightmare on Elm Street.

Roots of Joy

It took thirty-four winters
to finally laugh at the ice,
smile at the condensation escaping my lips,
whispering promises kept for myself.

I skip to my lou, embracing the views
of nature slumbering softly in the park.
Embark on this journey with my fingers
snapping in the cold rain
as disdain trickles down my raincoat of many
colors.
And, walk with pep in step while the snowflakes
dancing, hitting my face,
chit chat a playful reminder of the chill.

I embrace joy in this season too now.

Lessons From the Depth

Gave away my self-respect
for pain wrapped in disdain,
disguised as some long-term gain.

You were a hard lesson.
Sheesh!

Testing waters, you watched me drown,
pulling me out the millisecond death
was finna come scoop me.
My breath labored,
you reveled in my state of being.

Looks can be deceiving.

I was merely sleeping...
Or so my pride insists.

Either way,
screw you.

Glad to see you suffering,
ecstatic that your skies have turned gray,
once so vibrant and blue.

The deep healing I had to endure,
the valleys I clawed my way up,
monsters laughing at my wailing echoes...

51

You deserve every burden you're carrying.
I hope it anchors you to the sea floor,
never to harm another soul again.

Lemme Loneee.

You lost your supply.
So, you had your funky flying monkeys
do a fly-by of lurkin'.
You still really hurtin' over the damage *you* did?
The mind games, emotional cheatin', creepin'
with a dash of triangulation?

Years later, I'm grateful I walked away.
So, please lemme loneee.
They say you don't know what you got 'til it's
gone,
but your delusional self still doesn't see the
wrong.
That's fine.
Please lemme loneee.

It's a sad song, you still riffin' in my inbox,
still hummin' 'bout your slops and what nots

Keep your misery.
Keep your glittery pile of abuse.
Play obtuse over there.
I'm good over here.
Please lemme loneeeeeee.

Tardy Buddy

Keep your apologies.
You just want to offload your guilt.
Go sink in your own psychological consequences.

Vampire at the Circus

I remember doubting what my eyeballs revealed.
Tasting your words as truth,
as my eyes lingered at the facts,
craving to be seen FORREAL.
I apologized to *you*,
naively believing your gaslighting
was honesty on mute.
I swallowed your words.
I swallowed your lies only to
find the truth buried deep,
ready to cuss me out
and encourage me to wise the fuck up.

Called

Stomped on butterflies and called yourself a
menace.
Wrapped your arms around a predator and called
yourself civil.
Called yourself a hero when I told you no.
Called yourself a friend when she asked for
faithfulness.
What flavor of morality do you season over your
character?

Laughed at hurtful tears and called yourself safe.
Screamed viscerally at a victim's justice and called
yourself sound.

Denounced her cry for protection and called
yourself a doctor.
Embraced misery and called yourself a healer.
Called yourself wholesome when platforming
violators.

Made a joyful noise as the visionaries had their
ideals ripped from the top and pull down to the
very bottom until separation had a more sinister
meaning.

Created a tune for the emotional draculas to rock
to, snap their fingers and bite into their loved
one's neck with tears and accountability nowhere
on the dancefloor.

Devised a plan to eat everything you see
and blamed the world for allowing you to view
greed.

Greed was inspired *by* you.

Remember?

Too Sensitive, Said the MAB

I was often teased when I was a wee-thing
for being too sensitive by adults
who should have known better.

I was allowed to have hurt feelings—
as long as they remained hidden in the shadows.
Let it not be an adult that hurt my feelings,
and if I spoke up....
I was the problem.

Hearing lines like,
"Why'd you get left back? Too stupid, huh?"
At the age of 10 from a grown family member.
I was the problem.

Too sensitive.
Emotions too heavy for them to bear,
too burdensome for their fragile pride.
So, I decided I'd carried them myself...
Weights I thought I had to own.

Glad I stopped doing that.
I shed those kinds of shadows,
learned how to breathe in light.
I still speak up.
Or, let the door to my life closing
in their face be my voice.

Phantom Landmines and Lilies

It isn't betrayal.
But because of survival and upkeeping livelihood,
the sensation of an explosion to the heart,
feels like my insides have shattered...
Damage that will be memorialized.
Tears, hot and relentless,
mirror the gnawing twinge pulsing from my
belly,
as if it were indeed betrayal.

I am allowed to hate this.
I don't have to be understanding
but I can't help but understand.
To see how surviving
can sometimes hurt the ones you love the most.
And that maybe if you just
tip toe around the landmines
with flowers in your hand,
the proximity to being around the enemy
won't sting as much.

But it doesn't.

It bites...nibbles *around* the idea of a delicious
dishonest letdown.
And hot damn it's distasteful.
Fuck that:
It hurts.

Catching up With Unc'

He said it isn't natural.
He said it's not okay.
He said, "I don't blame her for not telling
anyone,
for keeping quiet,
because she's probably embarrassed."

He said, "If my daughter or son told me
something like that,
I would be devastated."
He said, "You hurt your mother.
She sacrificed so much for you,
and to find this out—
it hurts her."

But despite it all,
he still has faith that I'll return.
That I'll fall in line with being someone I am not.
Someone shamefully hidden in a closet
for his comfort, for her comfort too.
He still loves me,
and it's still my life.

So "true".
With that bullshit and that momentary truth,
stay over there and do you.

Learned the Dynamics in the Church House First

Big boy gotta eat.
So, lil' girl, starve.
Control your self-defense, lil' girl,
Big Boy has to harm.

He gotta eat all of the things
with the support of his family,
justifying all the mischief he brings,
appeasing his gluttony.

He gotta pull up other's roots
to wrap around his arms.
How else will he claim brilliance?
How else will he obtain resilience?
An early summer soft breeze makes his teeth
chatter.
So, during rainfall, he snatches growing stems as
the water pitter patters.
Consequence never touched Big Boy.
lil' girl, you need all the discipline for shielding
your anchors.

Big Boy livin' in the dangerous streets of the
suburbs.
He gotta cosplay your hood, lil' girl.

Big Boy gotta eat.

So, starve, lil' girl.
Control your voice, lil' girl.
The world will villainize you,
with charm stuck in their teeth, lil' girl.
Big Boy gets to harm.

Amnesia will be their choice of anecdote
when you grow up and mature.
They'll hide away from their past adult actions,
knowing accountability is the cure.

Praying to their god that you won't speak up,
asking their god for forgiveness,
while hoping you snag some forgetfulness.
Never giving you an apology,
hoping folks are distracted by your apostacy.

lil' girl, you ain't little no more.
The roots are solid,
and the rotten stems have been cut.
Talk yo' shit,
strut yo' stuff.

'Cause it's clear...
          they never really gave a fuck.

Bout it Bout it

I muted the cacophony daring to escape my
throat.
It wasn't pent up sounds of rage, no.
It was the freedom
from disrespect — acoustic.
I chose restraint to
keep it classy — out of spite.
The grass
under my bare feet
didn't deserve the earsplitting clamor.

You did though.

So, I sighed instead,
knowing that there was no
performance required when departing.

I let the earth fix my fear of letting go.
Let the buzzing bees distract my overthinking,
Permitted the chilly morning breeze whizzing
through the trees to whisk away mediocrity from
the root.
With phone in hand, you on the other end of the
line,
I exhaled it all away.
Let you talk about wondering if it's time to end.
'Cause while you was wonderin',
I was bout it.

Cleaning Out the Heart

I used to hold onto offenses,
a shield against their return.
But where do I place the refreshed joy,
love, and harmony?

How was I going to showcase
the beautiful support on my mantle
when a grudge from 2015 sprawls
across the marble slab,
chillin' above the fireplace?
Where would the lemon-fresh epiphanies go,
the shared laughter and comforting moments,
if resentment was cluttering every corner,
stinking up the joint like an unwelcomed guest?

So, I let it all go.
Them mofos still have no access though...
But I let the ache go.
Come on, newness!
Bring yo' ass in here, peace!

I've Known of the Rise

The glistening flickers of light jig over the
waters.
I call it a magical river,
a life source this land tries to dehydrate me from.
Heaven forbid I trust myself,
believing my heart to be far from deceitful.
This evening, I've made it my mission
to reunite with, and release, those waters.

There is a tug,
a slow pull at the base of my pelvis,
lifting,
raising,
reaching up my throat,
rushing past my tongue,
pushing against my teeth.

But Honey...
It's been so long since I felt it,
I mistook it for a hazardous swamp,
craving to drown anyone nearby.
I'd rather suffer alone than burden anyone else.
So just when I'm about to swallow it back down,
that magical river—
that glistening wave of action and guided
swirls—
sends a secondary wave,
bubbling up,
tsunamis up my chest,

giving my heart something to tremble about,
and flows from my lips.

I speak.
I speak of coral,
of desperate gurgles and thick morning mist.
I speak of storms I nearly drowned in,
storms I sailed through as if I knew the formula
for chaos.
I speak of loss,
I speak of love—
living with my head above water.
I speak of seaweed on seashells,
and fish swimming unafraid of predators.
I speak of the elders,
who know this enchanted river,
and refuse to let this land dry it out.
I speak of swimming onward,
floating on days when I wonder if anyone cares
to listen.
I speak of these waters—
these lifesaving, centering, calming,
warning and soothing waters...

Abscission, the Unsolicited Host.

Gripping the petals tightly — I tremble at the
unknown.
Still, dry petals slip away — it's inevitable.
It's time, yes.
But *ready* needs to pause.

I refuse to prepare.
I don't want a plan.

Comfort makes the sun feel warmer
and safety lingers right behind it.

I can make a real nice potpourri bowl.

For new to bloom,
the old must fall away,
release:
to be carried by the wind.
To tumble in territories that know nothing of
those petals' growth or journey.

I've always hated the "old must fall away" part.

Why can't I hold *new* in one hand,
old in the other, and *future* in my shirt pocket?

Gosh.

Journal #8027

In the quiet of the night,
I begin to stir.
Long live phoenixes,
our odyssey ain't nothin' to chuckle about.
But we giggle at how they believed our failures
were the end of us.

In the quiet of the night,
I begin to stir.
My heartbeat, a whisper,
an eye wink, a pact.
A tickering promise of rebirth.

Ashes of yesterday
confiscated with the helping hands
of wind and victory.
My wings ignited,
every feather a flame,
every beat a declaration of
freedom, power and evolution.

This is it—
The courage to soar,
to bow my head in honor of the soil,
to at last leave the ground
and fly under the wisdom of this new beginning.

This is it—
Right here.   I've been here before.
In this space.   This sacred space.
            I learned to rise here.
            Ignite my own flames here.
            Time to ascend.
            Ready for what's ahead.

Note to Self

You won't give it a rest and I'm so proud of you
for refusing to.
You pressed.
Pushed through.
Made it to the other side.
Never drowned, maybe sank a little.
Now you ride the waves during storms, go ahead,
show the improvement.
I rub my chest with appreciation.
Baby, it's good to be alive.
I strived, still strive but with love and grace in my
hands.
Oh, Jasmine,
I'm so glad you didn't give up on you.

Wings

Flight from Shadows

Rising from the soil,
soaring into the natural light...
I don't shun from the pangs or clutch tightly to
ancient delights.
I find balance in the blessings and plights.
Laugh at the lessons that had bite.
Tearful, "Thank you"s during the heights.
Regardless of circumstance,
my being always takes flight.

Wrong or right, my claws grip the earth firmly.
I learned about strife early.
Delayed the belief that I'm worthy.
Now, I see clearly.

Balance, Honey.
Balance.

Rising From the Soil, Soaring towards the Skies

Where pain whispered secrets,
I emerged,
a phoenix woven from scars,
each mark a testament
to battles fought in silence.
Betrayal lingered like a fog,
its chill wrapping around my spirit,
yet within that darkness,
a spark ignited,
the alchemy of my heart
transforming hurt into light.
Abandonment echoed,
but I learned to dance
with the ghosts of my past,
liberty jiggin'
to weave their stories
into the fabric of my being,
each thread a reminder
of my strength,
a fancy coat of resilience.

Heartbreak, an ugly bug-eyed teacher
with lessons carved in sorrow,
guided me to the well of bliss,
where I drew forth abundance,
not of things,
but of spirit and connection,

nourishing the roots of good lovin'
that blossomed within.

Now I soar,
I strut too,
a testament to the harsh journey,
arms wide open,
embracing the symphony of life,
where every note of struggle
has become a melody of freedom,
and joy dances in the light
of a heart unbound.

Flying

One day,
the sky refused to continue apologizing
for how much space it took up.
I decided that I could do the same.

Hell yeah, I woke up bright eyed and shimmying
in rainbow earrings, fury and boots.

But I didn't tear the closet door down
I just...
stopped saying "maybe."
Ceased praying for liberation
from what's actually freedom.
Stopped biting my tongue
when it whispered her name.

I wear my bookbags
and totes without my theme music.

No more folding into someone else's arms
like a polite lie.
Forget making space in my mouth
for words that don't fit.
I think about the women—
all the women—
who felt like the first deep breath
after too many held.
The ones who looked at me
like I was a watery reflection

and finally,
I looked back.

No one had to understand.
They still don't.

But when she smiled at me
like I was home,
I knew.
I wasn't confused.
I wasn't lost.
I was flying.
Unapologetic.
Expansive.
Yellow with the possibility of love.

Growing Free

You screamed with dogmatism,
"And you standing there unashamed when you
ought to be."
Once again, you dangled the fruit of acceptance,
hoping I'd bite the rotten fruit,
let the tangy juices of self-loathing run down my
chin,
and come running with open arms,
a heart ready to surrender
to your tarty sweet 'n' sour.

But I let it swing like a grandfather clock,
gave you a timeless smile as realization hit your
eyes,
your hands shook:

You have lost your grip on me.
My absence brings the mirror closer to you.

You condemned me to hell,
threatened devils and darkness,
but I stood resolute, unfazed,
a phoenix rising for the umpteenth time,
a wildflower blooming where you tried to plant
thorns.
Your anger was a storm I once feared,
but now, I wear my rain boots,
twirling in the downpour,
each drop a reminder of my grit.

You thought your attacks would tether me,
but I've grown sturdier roots
and your shadows no longer cast doubt.

I am unashamed, yes.
A garden thriving in the light of acceptance,
finding joy in the arms of another woman,
free from the chains of your disapproval.

So, let the winds howl and the storms rage,
for this flower has grown.
Not in your garden — but in my own,
and I am blooming beautifully, fiercely,
an anthem of elasticity,
a testament to the love that cannot be repressed.

I am unashamed, yes.

Liberty Jig

Shoulders unchained,
rocking to a bold bass.
My earrings tambourine play to the sounds of
my favorite jams.
Grandiose twirls,
circling in the kitchen
with white socks that have no business being
slipper-less.

I'm grown now.

I utter Lil Kim's cuss words with understanding.
Slow bouncing to Jill Scott
in honor of my younger knees
that used to discreetly dip low with beat drops.

I'm grown now.

Open palms raised to the ceiling,
feet anchored,
my hips tell passed-down fears to
Go on somewhere.

"Godly women don't move like that."
"Your earrings are too big."
"You just want to sin."

To go somewhere and stay put.

Ain't no melody for lack luster love, or regrets
crooning as I sway.

No.
Not in this kitchen.
Not in this liberty.

Embracing Balance With my Middle Finger Up

Somewhere within...
where shadows creep,
>   soundless whispers of secrets captured by
>   external misery-eaters to keep.

Days are eternal and nights further extend.
A heavy heart, abandoned, no hand to lend.

>   But
in the dark, a spark can glow,
>   a silky flicker, a chance to grow.

Over tangled thoughts, a voice will rise,
A clarifying truth underneath the skies.

Storms release their wildest roars.
Hope seems more absent than before.

Then a moment breaks—
Still somewhere within...
Illuminating everything.

Laughing collectively,
honoring the past betrayals respectfully.
Those fleeting seconds mean so much.
Serenity's echo grows louder; pain recedes.
A balm for my aching needs.

Forgiveness of self, forgiveness gifted to others.
The promise to refuse seeking confirmation from
another.
I was meant to pull off the covers of the plotters
undercover.

So, if the night ever feels, once again,
endless and cold,
I'll bow my head in gratitude, embracing the
power
of my shadow, the strength in righteous rage, the
lessons in grief,
the relief of releasing loved ones in their disbelief.

I'll remember the tales of bright...
    After every shadowed plight,
            My heart will find its way to
the other side:
                The light.

Late Bloomer Clicks

On January 25th, 2018, it clicked,
like high heels striking New York City concrete,
each step echoing my truth,
as if 7th Avenue and 24th Street
were made for my phoenix walk.
Not entirely sure of myself yet.
But I keep struttin',
switchin' my hips,
speaking with colorful tips.

On January 25th, it clicked—
a moment when something snapped back into
place,
securing the uncertainty at my red root.
I unpacked skeletal beliefs,
shame the size of 97 Nephilims,
and dimly lit romances
reflected in the eyes of those
who saw me as their lover.
I unearthed feelings of obligated attraction and
faux lust,
revealing stories hidden beneath my skin—
sandbox tales of a wife and two cats,
discreet red cheeks flushed in secrecy,
vines of memories entwining,
each one a treasure I'll never forget.

I've got stories under my skin—
women whom I've adored in silence,

to whom I'd offer my whole being if they asked.
Peel my heart open like ripe mangos in August
or Post-its left in prayer rooms.
After de-converting, I sought repentance,
relentless in my search for a cure
in a man,
longing for a "he" to dim the light in my eye
that sparkles for curvy silhouettes and sharp
tongues.
But I found no one.
My heart ached with an emptiness,
my soul bellowing in darkness
it didn't need to endure.

So, I unpacked.
Gave dogmatism the middle finger,
shared my simmering tales with friends,
and whispered the truth to my reflection.
Ain't no going back now.

Livin' Out Dat One Dream

No longer waiting,
anticipating the harvest,
the feast,
the dream I had years ago
about floating up from the bottom of the cement
stairs with ancient symbols,
into the high riser with the red trim
and up to the top floor...
is here.

I'm thankful for the slow and steady,
the quiet and 3am intrusive thoughts about never
giving up no matter what.

My mind has elevated, I've got a few wise tips,
a bag o' tricks to shove winter into a hole.
Returned to freely wearing my heart on my
sleeve.

This kind of height can never be taken away
from me.

Gripping the Echoes

Ignored sobs finally claw through my raspy
throat,
and release.
There's a silence, a pause after.

This that toddler cry.
Catching my breath after a big wail,
ready for round two of tears
salty enough to give Far Rockaway beach water
something to be weary of.

I thought I was over this.
I grip the memory, let it play—
No marination, no stewing or cooking up
shoulda, coulda scenarios.

I let it unfold.

Free the emotions

Give some more space for healing to get comfier.

'Cause you know...
                              Healing isn't linear.

Keep it Cute, Doubt

I wanna know what my heart sounds
like when the world attempts to annihilate
its melody to assist me in pursuing my dreams.

I wonder if it pauses or if it's tempted to
whimper at the world's fiery darts.
I wonder if it drowns out the sirens that "reality"
tries to sing to it.

I know my random gazes into the distance send
me
to the darkest moments of my life sometimes.

                              I know gratitude stares
                   right the fuck back.
                              Growth hates to see my
                              pretty ass comin'...

Rise Up Singin' Jasmine

Took me 10 years but I'm here.
With my rock, my honey bun, furry boss lady
and love that never runs dry.
Summertime feels like a *better* different now,
Holiday.
It's a good thing.
The living is easy now.

The Prodigal Jam

I knew the balm was settled in my soul
when I could play one of my favorite jams
without wincing at the pain our story
harmonized with,
without clenching my teeth
at the favor you vacuumed out of it.

The saxophone?
Back to a moan that nudged the joy
I've always carried but often forgot I had.
It wasn't just nostalgic blares—
this was a present reed,
mindful and robust like Coltrane,
warm and pop-like like Kenny.
Jazzy how I like it, Honey.

The guitar returned to its heart-serenading
strums.
Francesca glinged on a stage of flashbacks
I thought I'd never overcome.

The trumpets pushed beyond the past that
wounded
and settled in the instant I first discovered this
jam.
The lyrics were empowering once more;
her voice reminded me
of ease, love, and the beauty that grounds—
like it should have always been.

It was just one of my favorites again.

Sitcho Ass Down for a Minute

In the tempo of life, where the hustle hums,
I hear the call of drums.
But underneath the mass of society's insistence,
lies the consecrated art of my own existence.
                                        Rest.
A revolution, a powerful stance,
a soft rebellion against the endless dance.
In quiet moments, I reclaim my grace,
finding solace in stillness, a sacred space.
The world may demand I push and strive.
                                        Fuck that.

It's in the gentle pauses that I truly thrive.
Strength ain't merely in what I achieve,
it's knowing when to pause, when to breathe.
                                        Breathe.

With each deep breath, I dismantle the rush,
embracing my worth in a soft, tender hush.

In rest, I find power.
                                        In stillness, I rise.

Nurturing myself, I uplift the whole.

Rest is my anthem:
                                        a balm for my soul.

Her Silly Little Timeline

Me and my silly little timeline...
Summer in February,
Spring in September.
Kinky with T through every transition,
putting me in positions I'm...
Nevermind.

Me and my silly little timeline...
Dropping when I want,
writing when I please,
creating at all times—
no one will ever be appeased.
This is about what needs to be released.

Me and my silly little timeline...
The city burns while I chill,
T-shirt and panties,
frosty fingers, chilly legs.
May felt like winter—
hot damn, it was rigid.

Me and my silly little timeline...
I stand,
unbothered and bold,
sashaying through seasons,
letting the stories unfold.
I'll let the flames flicker,
allowing seasons to collide,

accepting my beautiful mess
and enjoying the ride.

Me and my silly little timeline:
where I truly belong.

It's Nice on This Side Too, Honey

Girl...
Lemme just go 'head and *let* life be good.
Let life show me how safe it is to
bask in happiness,
shine in who I am,
bathe in long laughter with friends
and, give the present a real good look.
            Nah, I'm playin'

I *choose* life to be good.
I *choose* to laze about in happiness with my
house shoes on,
shine in the me I know best,
Breathe slowly in tear-eyed cackles
while knowing the present is a safe spot
to rub my feet together in.

            Pfft, *let.*
Please...

No Access

In the spot — I finally got it right
and hot damn it's bright
and I'll leave the remaining gems on the front
steps outta spite.
Let you think speaking wrong on me was right.
Let you believe your slithering green would thrive
without a fight.

Look at you.
No access.

You bangin' on the front door of my theater
with the "Remember me?" screech and your
hands ready to leech.
The same hands that were slow to reach out and
help me. The same lips that preached about
doing and your actions lacked traction when it
came to supporting me.

No access.
But let her tell it.

She was there; she just forgot the receipts.
She forgot I too needed a support beam,
a sturdy line of encouragement when I thought it
was time to exit stage left.
When I thought the ashes of the past were swept.
When I thought I released all the pain I kept.
You were absent.

No access.
No access.
No access.

Ain't Self-Made

I'm here because my parents made me,
here because Grandma and Grandpa nurtured my
creativity,
with a little fussin'—mostly from Grandma.
I'm here because Mama
mmhm'd my baby jargon,
yeah'd at my scribblings,
and Daddy wouldn't let up
his affirmations, rock solid, a fortress of support.
I've got aunties and uncles who accept me for me,
friends who loved me down to the dregs,
when all I could afford was tea.
Now I can splurge on maybe two biscuits.
Biscuit...
We're always in tune,
even with different lyrics—
out of sync but harmonizing,
as life flows on and on.
Do you hear it, Lee?

I'm free to be me because of an example like
Alivey...
I smile at past giggles shared, my voice always
bare when she was there to listen.
"The pretty one" with the hangtime, honey bee
streaks.
And where would I be without my sister, Nique?
Whether we speak for weeks or years,

97

I wouldn't be here without her listening ear,
her unwavering presence, my anchor in the storm.

I'm here because Muffin knew I could do
nothing but write
before anything else.
She'd sit there, reading lines,
interpreting the spaces in between,
fussin' over my reluctance to share my crevices.
Because if I'm gonna share my heart,
I might as well bleed it all out in ink.

I'm here because Mama B wouldn't let me be
weak. Her softness in voice, power in tongue.
I see where Char got it from—
She pulled me out of my shell,
wrapped me in a cloak of patience,
kept me warm, safe from unprovoked scorn.

I know what I was born to do,
but I wouldn't be here without you—yes, you,
dear reader.
You paid to read my thoughts,
in poetry form and messy novelin'.
You, who reads my lines,
finding pieces of yourself in my words
(hopefully).
And T, well, that was just fate.
I wouldn't be here without their grace,
love, and smiles.
So glad we get to walk this path together,

or at least for a long while.

I'm here because my community saw me for me,
and remained—
Ain't a thing about me self-made.

Genevieve Tha Mighty God Sis

I'll never miss you — you're always with me...
That lingering smile when one of *our* jams play.
The tunes that made *us* slide in *our* socks with grace,
clumsy diva-in-the-making spins.

You're in the grins of our inside jokes,
crafted during moments when pain thought it could win.

You'll never miss me — I'm always with you...
Simmering underneath the off-key notes of a passerby
when you're on your way to wherever.
You know I still think I've got Whitney Houston vocals.
Though truth be told, I sing with the flavor of
four pigeons, combined with 3 alley cats in heat.

When life pulls — I'm pushing *with you* to get through.
When life tries to drown — you're fussin' *with me* to remember I can float.

I know about being protective of myself — you were always so protective of me.
                              It was reciprocal.
Walking shields for *each other* — the ache was
forever real when we missed a spot.

Now, we're with each other in spirit on
Sundays...
Like when we'd walk to the store to snag treats
in-between services.
Fried crab legs were a dolla back then.
The Chinese food spot is now an Applebees.

We still sisters no matter what changes around
us.

Now, we're with each other in spirit during
summertime walks...
Like when Mt. Vernon's 4th avenue was our
everything.
Pretty Girl,
Fabco,
That record store...
I purchased my first CD with my own money on
4th avenue.
Voyage to India by India Arie.
You got Lil Jon's *Crunk Juice*
Rememba?

The way I had to hide that Cd from my mama,
girl...

You'd always fuss with me to live a little.
I'd fuss and say you livin' too much.

In the end...

You were right.

I've been catching up with the livin part.
                    You were right.
Hmph.

I'm always there.
                    And you....
You're always here.

The Pretty One

Multi-faceted gem and free-flowing,
supporting my past poetry readings, writings and
books, you lifted my soul.
Not one to sugarcoat, you hold me in check,
you challenge my choices, ensure I reflect.

In 2017's darkness, when I lost my way,
you offered your perspective, helped me face the
day.
Though time stretches thin, and our talks are
hella rare,
you sit in my heart, a love beyond compare.
From college days bright to past journeys we
faced,
your truth, unapologetic, guided me to my own
grace.
With laughter and kindness, you can lift your
folks up each day,
rooting for dreams in your own special way.
was one of my anchors, reminding me of life.

Here's to our friendship, a bond strong and true.
Near or far, talk every day or a few years,
I cherish you always.

Do Me a Favor

I've seen you cook smiles.
In your speech, hoot spices of joy.
Season winces with giggles, you'd wiggle your
toes
until the storm surrendered to your spirit.
You were irrepressible.

Always held your arm out to receive.
You were always so needy.
Always so giving.
Freefalling on forgiveness and courage.
You clapped your hands and summoned
chaos to enter your courts
when your eyes still glistened
fresh water innocent.
You were golden.

You left this earth with voices still
chanting for your untarnished yellow,
your curved lines,
your bad choices,
your scary decisions,
your incision to everything
unfathomed and everything dangerous.
Your aura shined.
I've got a favor for us women
you've left behind:

Tell the clouds that you'll give them your heart.

Whisper your strength into the winds
and hurricane love until our hearts
shimmy out of the shells we created
from pseudo love.
Soothe the heavy spirits of women like me.

I've seen you cook smiles.
In your speech, cackle spices of joy.
Season winces with giggles, you'd wiggle your
toes
until the storm surrendered to your spirit.
You were irrepressible.
So, I know, you can hurricane love.

It's Forever with You

It's forever with you, nothing less.
We'll undress the fears that never belonged to us.
No need to throw them in the hamper—
let's burn the cloaks of ignored sores in the
backyard.
Let the wind carry the ashes of threaded terrors,
never to be seen again.
We'll kill time with machetes,
challenging who even made up that concept
anyway.
Gaze upon the past with gratitude,
give our hard-earned lessons honorable curtsies,
and gift the present the good stuff—
            you know, our attention.

We'll slow down,
taste the moments that make us laugh,
savor the head-back cackles,
the knee-slapping snickers.
Roll our eyes at the times we thought
the valley would be our home.
Roam around with our bare feet on the pulse,
the core,
the everything all at once,
and give thanks.
It's forever with you, nothing less.
It's vacations and stay-ins,
dry spells and silence that feels like warm
brownies

after OG Kush beyond 11PM.
It's sending sabotage to the gallows
and summoning a jester to remind us
how our egos can be so trivial sometimes.
It's saying what's on our chest
while remembering both parties have a heart
underneath.
It's growth,
it's change.
It's closed chapters and new stories.
It's forever with you, nothing less.

Naddy the Focus Pocus

There is this thing you do with the tips of your
fingers and our hair oil potion.
Bubble, bubble, massage my beautiful coils
without trouble.
Circular tenderness removing
the curse of dry soil
and decompressing the toiling of regression.

There's magic in your hands.

Years of committed conjuring of 100,000
follicles to be upkept.
Defying gravity, your fingers whisper spells
of love, devotion and acceptance.

There's magic in your hands.

Monumental Mervyn and His Princess

In the mirror's light, way before the age of 5,
he'd lift me high,
"Who is that pretty girl?" he'd ask, eyes bright,
"My Princess," he'd declare, with warmth in his
sigh.
A gentle affirmation, my spirit took flight.

Through the years, he's changed, evolved like a
song,
from busy shadows to a heart that's serene,
patient and kind, where I've always belonged,
in his laughter, I found my dreams gleaned.

Road trips to nowhere, laughter in the air,
he'd pick me up, always present, always there.
With every question I tossed, he'd pause and
care,
in every moment shared, love woven with flair.

When the world felt heavy, his strength held me
close.
In sickness, in sorrow, he's the anchor I chose.
A rock through the storms, in joy and in woes.
His unwavering support, a garden that grows.

At my performances, pride in his eyes,
a camera held steady, capturing my rise.
With every word spoken, he'd help me be wise.
In my voice, in my heart, his love never lies.

"Embrace who you are," he said, voice so clear,
in the face of the teasing, he banished my fear.
For the things that make us, we should hold dear.

Through every season, his love's been my guide,
in laughter, in trials, he's stood by my side.
With wisdom and kindness, in him I confide.
Monumental Mervyn, my father, my pride.

So, here's to the man who's shaped who I am,
with each step I take, I carry his plan.
In this journey of life, I'll always stand,
as his princess forever, hand in hand.

WILMG II

Your absence no longer pangs beneath my chest.
I smile at your memory.
Shake my head at what I think you would say
whenever I'm misaligned.
Tear up when using your recipes.
Your presence is felt in the little things...
But I'll always long for you during the big things.

Time ain't heal shit.

Auntie Mo

You forever summer season,
sun beamin' on dreams to never give up
and self-respect that stands unwavering:
                    I love you.

You've tucked some of my secrets in your jean
pockets,
a few jokes echo in my mind,
your impact lives warmly in my heart.

You just keep going...
I watch in awe, pride swelling within.
What can't you do?
                    You can't give up.
                    You can't give in.

Harsh wisdom wrapped in gentle advice,
I never think twice when I come to you,
knowing, without fail, it'll be just what I need.

I don't have favorites...
But if you ever met any of the people I dated,
it's because I envisioned a future with them.
If I ever thought of you,
gratitude would fill the air,
for having a loved one like you.

I don't have favorites...
But if I ever won the lottery in the millions,
you'd know about it with a stash handed to you.

Auntie Mo,
you blooming bed of lavender,
grit and honeysuckle in a realm where peace and
serenity play freeze tag:
                    I love you.

A Descent into Light's Embrace

Self-Renewal
I let compassion kiss my spirit...
Gifted myself the people, places, and things I
need.
Saying "No" became my new priority.
No more pleading to pour myself empty.
No more surrounding myself by those who chose
not to pour into me.
Instead, I pour back into myself.
Mindfulness knows my name now.
A lifelong process, and I embrace it.

Grace
Lil' Jasmine hollers reminders from the recesses
of my mind:
"Satdown somewhere!"
I surrender to my humanity,
laughing as my quintessence rolls her eyes
at outlandish expectations.
I take it easy; I'm worth this ease—I know it
now.

Patience
Speaking of sattin' down...
Under a big tree, I joined the "Time is a Social
Construct" club.
My T-shirt arrived, perfectly on time.
Abandoned the desire to place deadlines on goals
and reunited with flow.

I hold my timelines loosely.
Focus is swirling in my eyes.

Loyalty
I show up for my core values,
celebrating small wins with the same joy as the
big ones.
Me and my intuition chit-chat all the time,
and I actually listen now.
No longer believing that time equals quality.
I cherish the solid friendships, both new and old.

Poetry is... Part II

Back in the day...
I scrawled dreams in secret places,
scribble-scrabble on memo pads,
in my late grandmother's room,
where joy mingled with rebellion.
Each word a whisper,
each story a song,
my mother nodding,
as if Langston Hughes
had reached Grandma's Brooklyn home,
a language of toddlers,
full of wonder.
But poetry pinched,
like clothes pins on laundry lines,
in second grade's classroom,
where innocence felt fragile.

When I was a preteen, age thirteen,
angst bubbled,
secrets tangled in my heart,
love unreturned,
"No one never understands."
I needed an outlet,
a place to release my feelings,
stacks of notebooks filled,
with unfiltered thoughts.

Fashion dreams danced,
stitching glamour and sketches,

but in class, my pen took over,
verses flowed like fabric.
Through The Hanger,
my spirit ignited,
a poetry event,
voices rising like thunder,
each story a heartbeat,
truths spilling forth.
I watched students speak,
'bout gold diggers and bossy bitches,
their words weren't resonating,
but it was still solid,
sparking something deep inside.
I knew then,
I wanted to share my journey,
to write my own truth.
Now, as I navigate this path,
with eight collections born
from whispered struggles,
to an evolved Jasmine in bloom,
I found my voice in poetry,
a canvas for my heart.
My wounds and wisdom,
love tales and strife,
each verse a piece of me,
a memoir in motion.
I will weave my words
with every passing year,
experimenting, exploring,
finding light in the lines,
where my soul can soar free.

Hell nah, I ain't stopping.
Poetry lives and breathes in me.

The Writing Witch

A cedar wand wields an unassuming power.
Capturing impossible by its strength.
The embedded granite alchemizes something
serious.

The New Garden

In a garden once vibrant, where we once thrived,
a shadow took root, where the sunlight arrived.
A flower, once blooming, now wilted with fear,
its petals, like whispers, drew sorrow near.
Hpmh.

The thorns of ya' doubt wound tight 'round your
heart, in the soil of ya' mind, we began to part.

I tended my boundaries, like walls made of stone,
safeguarded the blossoms that flourished alone.
In this new luscious garden, I had to forgive,
the weeds of resentment needed to no longer live.
Beneath every thorn, there's a seed yet to grow.
And love's gentle rain can wash pain away slow.

Though paths may now wander, like rivers they
flow, I wish you the sunlight, the warmth that ya'
sow.

I'll cherish the colors, though some friendships
don't last.
Nope.

So, bloom where you're planted, in fields *far* and
wide.
May ya' heart find the courage, and hope be ya'
guide.

In this new luscious garden, I let go, but love will remain:
A reminder that healing can flourish from pain.

Flowers and Gifts

Check the name tag.
My fragrance ain't always sweet.
My petals don't always captivate.
My flaws stay showin'
and my defenses can be sour,
but when I'm sweet—
ain't no difference between me and sugar cane.
Ain't no sham in my sugar, Suga.
Pink lily, sensitive soul.
Thirteen years later,
I still wallow like white lilies
in winter winds for Grandma.
Willow tree sways in my walk,
I treat poetry like sassafras—
each petal unique, none the same.
As seasons change, my roots stay sturdy.

Roots and Wings

I am a phoenix.
I am a flower.
Rising from the ashes,
blooming in June.
Soaring through the skies
with fire in my eyes,
swaying delicately
in the early morning breeze.

I've been set ablaze hella times,
seen a shit ton of darkness in the dirt.
I've curtsied at the edges of over
and never tipped,
lowered my head, ready for death,
but rebirth told me to rise.

I've cried in puddles
where sleep was a hearty blink,
for deep slumber was a danger
for someone who faced winter
for over 365 days and a stint.
I remember pulling lint from my pants
like love me or love me nots
to better days.

I am a phoenix,
opened my beak for Trazodone,
deep journaling, and T reminding me
of the wings I can always use to fly.

I am a phoenix.
I remember.
I know resilience.

But I also know joy,
even if I'm blindfolded,
underwater, with my hands
and ears clogged.
It's soft petals unplucked,
it's lessons learned,
truth rediscovered at the roots and purpose rising
through cumulus,
an odyssey just giving the sky its sass without
fuss.

It's relief and gratitude.
It's effortless existence
and I'm finna bask all up in it.

About Jasmine Farrell

Jasmine Farrell, from Brooklyn, NY is an author, French-fry stealer to her loved ones and a snacker. Avid reader and married cat lady, Jasmine has loved writing since she was a wee-thing. With poetry being her first love, she has published five full-length poetry collections and one three-part poetry series. She recently published, *Rising From The Roots* (2025). Beyond writing, Jasmine Farrell embarked on a transformative journey of self-discovery. Today, she embraces her newfound self-awareness alongside her loving spouse and their delightful cat, Aubry. Through books, travel, cherished moments, and the magic of live theater, Jasmine Farrell finds joy and fuels her creativity.

Check Out My Other Books:

Orange September – 2023

Sloppy (A novel) – 2022

Release: *YOU* – 2020

Release: *Love Defamed* – 2020

Release: *Cycles* - 2020

Let's Connect:

Personal Website:
http://www.jasminefarrell.com

YouTube:
@JasmineFarrell

Social Media:
TikTok: @Jasminefarrellpoetry
Instagram: @authorjfarrell

Thank you.

9 781737 946076